Gary Paulsen

Prince Amos

A YEARLING BOOK

Published by
Dell Publishing
a division of
Bantam Doubleday Dell Publishing Group, Inc.
1540 Broadway
New York, New York 10036

ISBN: 0-440-40928-4

Printed in the United States of America

March 1994

10 9 8 7 6 5 4 3 2 1

OPM

Prince Amos

OTHER YEARLING BOOKS YOU WILL ENJOY:

THE COOKCAMP, *Gary Paulsen*
THE VOYAGE OF THE *FROG*, *Gary Paulsen*
THE BOY WHO OWNED THE SCHOOL, *Gary Paulsen*
THE RIVER, *Gary Paulsen*
THE MONUMENT, *Gary Paulsen*
HOW TO EAT FRIED WORMS, *Thomas Rockwell*
HOW TO FIGHT A GIRL, *Thomas Rockwell*
HOW TO GET FABULOUSLY RICH, *Thomas Rockwell*
CHOCOLATE FEVER, *Robert Kimmel Smith*
BOBBY BASEBALL, *Robert Kimmel Smith*

YEARLING BOOKS/YOUNG YEARLINGS/YEARLING CLASSICS are designed especially to entertain and enlighten young people. Patricia Reilly Giff, consultant to this series, received her bachelor's degree from Marymount College and a master's degree in history from St. John's University. She holds a Professional Diploma in Reading and a Doctorate of Humane Letters from Hofstra University. She was a teacher and reading consultant for many years, and is the author of numerous books for young readers.

For a complete listing of all Yearling titles, write to Dell Readers Service, P.O. Box 1045, South Holland, IL 60473.

Prince Amos

Chapter · 1

Duncan—Dunc—Culpepper was in his room, choosing a tie to go with his new blue suit. "Amos, do you realize that we are about to become a part of history in the making?"

Amos Binder, his best friend for life, was sprawled across Dunc's bed, pulling little threads out of the bedspread.

"She loves me. She loves me not."

"Did you hear me, Amos? When we get to the state capitol tomorrow, we'll be able to witness firsthand how laws are made. It's really an honor to get to be a page for a senator. While we're running errands, we'll

1

get to see how the whole process works up close. . . . Amos?"

Dunc walked over and jerked the edge of his bedspread out of Amos's hand.

Amos scowled. "You made me land on 'she loves me not.'"

"You're ruining my bedspread. Aren't you even a little excited about getting to go to the state capitol to run errands for the senators?"

"Oh . . . that."

Dunc waved his hand in front of Amos's face. "Earth to Amos. What's with you today?"

Amos sat up. "Everybody in Mrs. Wormwood's social studies class is going to the state capitol, right?"

"Right."

Amos grinned. "Then that means Melissa called me last night."

Dunc shook his head. "I'm not following you."

"She knows I'm going."

"So?"

"So last night she called to tell me she

wanted to sit together on the bus and probably eat all her meals with me, and maybe get closer to me, and—"

Dunc raised one eyebrow. "Wait a minute. Melissa Hansen actually called you and told you all that?"

Amos had been in love with Melissa since the first day he met her in grade school, when he spilled chocolate milk down the back of her dress in the cafeteria.

"Not exactly. But she did call, and that's the important thing. We can work out the details on the bus tomorrow."

"What did she say?"

"It's kind of a long story. My family was in the living room, watching a football game. Uncle Alfred was sitting in his favorite chair. You remember Uncle Alfred?"

Dunc nodded. "The one that picks his feet through his stinky socks?"

"Right," Amos continued. "Anyway, everybody was in there watching the game. Actually, I was watching my cousin little Brucie. He's teething now, and he was chewing on Scruff's tail. It was really a better show than the TV. Scruff reached around and took a bite out of Brucie. Then Brucie grabbed Scruff's ear, and—"

"Amos, what did Melissa say?"

"Oh, yeah. Well, the phone rang just as the quarterback snapped the ball. Of course, I always take the shortest route to the phone. Melissa likes me to get it on that all-important first ring."

Dunc nodded again. Amos had this strange idea that Melissa would hang up if he didn't get to the phone by the first ring. In the past Dunc had tried to reason with him. Tried to explain that since Melissa Hansen had never once in her entire life called Amos, he couldn't possibly know what ring she wanted him to answer on. But he couldn't convince him and had finally given up trying.

"I stepped up onto the coffee table," Amos went on, "missed all the dips and snacks, and had a clear shot at the phone. My form was excellent, rhythm and timing perfect. My left foot was powering off the coffee table. I was about to hit the core stride when it happened."

4

"What?"

"I blocked Uncle Alfred's view of a touchdown. He grabbed me in midair as I stepped off the table and tossed me into the metal trash can in the corner of the room. It was amazing. You wouldn't think a man that big could move that fast. He was back in his chair before the announcer finished calling the play."

"Did you make it to the phone?"

"No. It took my mom almost an hour to pry the trash can off my rear end."

"Then who talked to Melissa?"

"Little Brucie. But he bit the telephone cord in two before anyone could get to the phone."

"You never talked to her, but you know she wants to sit with you?"

Amos grinned. "Yeah. Isn't it wonderful?"

Chapter·2

Dunc turned the key in the door of the motel room. "I'm sorry it didn't work out for you to sit with Melissa, Amos."

Amos plopped onto the nearest bed. "Why do teachers always have to make you sit in alphabetical order? It must be something they learn in teacher school. You probably can't graduate unless you sign something stating you promise to seat every future student alphabetically."

"Don't worry. I think you managed to get Melissa's attention anyway."

Amos sighed. "I don't want to talk about it."

"It might have been better if you had just waved from where you were sitting and not stood up in the seat. That way the driver wouldn't have pulled over and yelled at you."

"I said I didn't want to talk about it."

Dunc continued. "And I really think you went too far when you took your T-shirt off and used it as a flag to signal her."

Amos rolled over.

"Probably the worst thing was when you crawled under the seats, trying to get to Melissa, and you miscounted and came up under Mrs. Wormwood's dress. She was really serious about sending you home until I told her you were looking for my contact lens. I hope she doesn't find out that I don't wear contacts."

Amos sat up. "Thank you so much for giving me a review of this morning's events. You've really made me feel so much better. Now I know beyond a shadow of a doubt that Melissa thinks I am a complete dweeb."

Dunc shrugged. "I was just trying to tell you that I think Melissa noticed you. She probably thinks you're interesting. Kind of unique. Girls go for guys that are out of the ordinary."

"You think so?"

"Absolutely."

Amos jumped off the bed and headed for the door.

"Where are you going?"

"To Melissa's room. I'm going to try out my John Wayne impressions on her."

Dunc grabbed his arm. "Hold on. We have to be at the legislative building in ten minutes. Besides, I think you've given Melissa enough to think about for one day."

"Maybe you're right. I'll let her take it all in and spring the impressions on her at breakfast."

Dunc took his suit out. "Aren't you going to get dressed?"

Amos shook his head. "I think I'll wear what I have on."

"Mrs. Wormwood said we have to wear a suit. All legislative pages wear suits and ties."

"My mom did buy me a suit but we had to have the pants shortened. She gave it to a tailor at our dry cleaners. That's when the little switch happened."

"What switch? Just put on the suit. We're running out of time."

"When she went to pick up my suit, the cleaners had made a mistake, and they'd given it to someone else. The only other suit they could find that would fit me was the one Herbie Pittman wore when he played the part of a banana in the summer festival of fruit last year." Amos pulled a bright yellow suit out of his bag.

Dunc stared at the suit. He tried to think of something positive to say. Nothing came to him.

Amos's shoulders drooped. "That's what I thought too. How would it look if I clipped a tie on the front of my T-shirt?"

"It's a toss-up, but I think you're stuck with the suit. One thing about it—you'll be easy to find."

Chapter·3

Mrs. Wormwood led the group of students inside the carved double doors. She motioned for them to sit in the balcony. The first afternoon they were supposed to watch the session, and tomorrow they would begin their duties as official pages.

Heads turned as Amos made his way down the aisle. He had chosen a black tie to go with his yellow suit, and he looked like a large walking banana with a rotten place in the front.

Dunc took notes for the full hour. Amos slept through most of it.

When the last senator was through speaking, Dunc shook Amos's elbow. "Wake up. It's time to meet the senators we've been assigned to work with all week. Come on."

Amos rubbed his eyes. "I wasn't asleep. I was just resting my eyelids. Long trip and everything." He yawned and followed Dunc to the floor of the capitol building.

Dunc looked at the list. "You've been assigned to Senator Suborn, and I have Senator Grafter. There's mine." Dunc pointed to a tall white-haired man with a potbelly. "You look for yours. I'll meet you back here in a few minutes."

Amos wandered down the steps. His senator didn't seem to be around. He turned to climb back up the steps and nearly ran into a boy wearing a wide purple ribbon across his chest.

The boy stared at Amos. Amos stared back. They stayed like that. Staring for several minutes. Finally Amos blinked. He couldn't believe it. Looking at the boy was like looking in a mirror. They could have passed for identical twins.

The boy clicked his heels together and bowed. "I am Gustav the Eighth, Crown Prince of Moldavia. My entourage is here in America on a goodwill tour."

Amos stuck out his hand. "I'm Amos the First, Nintendo king of the greater United States. I'm here because my social studies teacher threatened to flunk me if I stayed home. Nice to meet you, Gus."

Dunc walked up as they were shaking hands. He looked from one face to the other and back again. "This is incredible. Amos, did you know that you two look exactly—"

Amos nodded. "Good-looking guy, isn't he? Dunc, meet Gus. Gus, this is my best friend, Dunc."

The boy clicked his heels again. "It is my extreme pleasure. I wonder, would the two of you do me the great honor of having breakfast with me tomorrow morning in my penthouse? It seems we have a great deal in common. I have a small proposition I'd like to discuss with you."

"Sorry," Amos started, "I'm all set to do my John Wayne impressions for—ouch!"

He glared at Dunc. "You almost broke my foot."

Dunc smiled. "We'd be happy to have breakfast with you, Your Highness. Thank you for asking."

"Fine. I will expect you at seven-thirty sharp. My hotel is the one across the street. Take the elevator to the top." The boy bowed one last time and left.

"You better have a good explanation for what you just did, or I'm going to rearrange your face," Amos growled.

"Amos, you can't turn down an invitation from a prince."

"For Melissa, I can turn down anybody."

"Mrs. Wormwood said Melissa's not feeling well. She may have the flu. I doubt if she'll even be at breakfast."

"Maybe I should take breakfast to her. You know, comfort her in her hour of need. She'd respect me, and then want me to be closer to her. . . ."

"Mrs. Wormwood is staying with her. She'll be fine. Besides, think how impressed she'll be when she finds out that you had breakfast with a real prince."

14

Amos looked thoughtful. "You might have a point there."

Dunc smiled. "Sure I do. Trust me."

"Don't push it."

Chapter·4

Amos stepped inside the elevator. "I sure hope Gus has something good for breakfast. I'm starved."

Dunc punched the button. "Can you imagine? We're going to have breakfast in a penthouse with a real live prince. Now aren't you glad you came with me?"

"I've been giving that some thought. Melissa would have been grateful to me for a long time if I had brought breakfast to her room. No telling how grateful."

"I told you she has the flu," Dunc said. "If you had brought her breakfast, she would

17

have thrown it up and it would have been all your fault."

"Melissa can't throw up," Amos said. "She isn't the kind who throws up. Girls like Melissa never throw up."

The elevator stopped at the top floor, and the boys stepped out. There was only one door.

"This must be the place." Dunc moved to the door and knocked.

A man wearing a black and white uniform opened the door. "Yes?" He stared at Amos.

Amos ducked under the man's arm into the spacious room. "We're here to see Gus."

The man moved to the side. "Prince Gustav, your . . . guests have arrived."

"Please show them in, Charles." The prince was seated at a table, poring over the front page of the morning newspaper.

He stood up and invited them to sit. "I didn't know what foods you liked, so I took the liberty of ordering one of everything on the menu. Please take your choice."

Amos lifted the lid off the French toast. "This prince business must pay pretty well."

Prince Gustav smiled. "I guess I do all right."

Dunc scooped out some scrambled eggs. "You mentioned something about a proposition?"

"My father is in Washington visiting with your president. He has sent me here as a goodwill ambassador. He will join me when he is finished in Washington."

"Okay." Dunc shrugged. "But what does this have to do with us?"

"I'm coming to that. Since I have been in your state, I haven't been allowed to address the legislature. Something always happens to prevent it. One night, Charles and I were locked in our room. Another time our limousine was delayed just long enough for me to miss an appointment. We have become the laughingstock of your country." He showed them an article on the front page of the newspaper.

Amos swallowed a bite of pancake. "Sounds to me like someone is going to a lot of trouble to make you look bad."

The prince nodded. "That's what Charles and I think. And here's where we need your

19

help. You may have noticed the uncanny resemblance we bear to each other?"

Amos looked at Dunc. "Is that another way of saying we look alike?"

Before Dunc could answer, the prince went on. "I propose that Amos and I trade places. Only for a short time. Until I can discover who is at the bottom of this conspiracy to discredit my country."

Dunc shook his head. "It would never work. Amos doesn't know anything about being a prince."

Amos wiped the milk off his face with the back of his hand. "Speak for yourself. I think I'd make a great prince."

Dunc frowned. "Amos, what about Mrs. Wormwood and the senators we've been assigned to work for?"

The prince cleared his throat. "All of that is easily taken care of. I will work for Amos's senator. It will be the perfect cover. And your teacher need never know. What do you say?"

"What about the butler?" Amos whispered.

"Charles is completely loyal to the

throne. He will go along with anything I ask. I have discussed the matter with him, and he is quite willing to help you play the part."

"Would I get to stay in the penthouse?"

"Of course. We would need to completely swap personalities. I will take your place as a page, and you will make a few small public appearances on my behalf. When we have this little matter cleared up, we will switch back."

"I don't think—" Dunc started.

"It's for his country," Amos interrupted. "It'll be tough living up here in luxury while you guys are down there slaving away—but I'm willing to make the sacrifice."

Chapter · 5

"Where have you been?" Mrs. Wormwood was waiting for them outside their motel room. She grabbed the prince by the ear and twisted. "I told you to stay with the group."

The prince gently but firmly removed her hand. "My dear lady. There's no need for alarm. My companion and I have simply been taking the morning air."

Mrs. Wormwood's mouth fell open.

Dunc took the prince's arm and pulled him inside the motel room. "Uh—he means we're real sorry, Mrs. Wormwood. We won't let it happen again."

The prince brushed an imaginary crumb off his sleeve. "What a difficult person."

Dunc scratched his head. "I think you better have a crash course in being Amos, or we could be in some serious trouble here."

"Did I do something wrong?"

"Well, it's just that Amos is a little more laid back. You know, less formal."

"I see. Is there anything else?"

"You've got to quit being so neat. Amos is sort of casual—in a sloppy kind of way."

"I'm afraid I don't understand."

"Let me show you." Dunc recombed the prince's hair so that it was flat on one side and stood up on the other. Then he took Amos's suit jacket, wadded it up, and sat on it.

The prince put it on and looked at himself in the mirror. "Your friend certainly has strange taste."

Amos was watching the big-screen TV in the penthouse. He had already ordered room service three times and was thinking about calling them again.

"Ahem." Charles cleared his throat. "I

hate to bother you, sir. But His Highness has an engagement in the Crystal Room at Wilshire Park in one hour. I think you should dress."

Amos looked down at himself. "I am dressed. This is the suit Gus had on. What's wrong with it?"

"The engagement will require a more formal attire, sir. I have your clothes laid out for you in the dressing room."

Amos pressed the off button on the remote control. "I guess it won't hurt me to change clothes."

He moved to the dressing room. Charles followed. Amos looked at him. "Did you leave something in here?"

"No, sir. I'm here to assist you."

"I don't know how things are in your country, Chuck, but where I come from, a guy my age dresses himself."

Charles bowed. "As you wish, sir. I'll be just outside if you need me."

Amos looked at the clothes lying on the couch. He picked up a piece of gold braid. "How hard can it be?"

Chapter · 6

Charles coughed and covered his mouth with his hand. "Might I suggest, sir, that you not wear your cummerbund on your head? It goes around the waist."

Amos pulled it off his head. "It's a belt? I would never have guessed! I figured it was either a hat or a slingshot."

"May I?" Charles fastened the black elastic piece around Amos's waist. "Might I also suggest that you comb your hair before we depart?"

Amos touched his hair. "I hate to break it to you, Chuck, but I already combed it."

Charles sighed. "Yes, sir. Would you mind terribly if I touched it up a bit?"

"You can try."

Twenty-five minutes and a jar of hair grease later, Amos was finally ready.

"There." Charles was obviously pleased with himself. "No one would ever guess you're not the prince."

Amos blew a big pink bubble. It popped and stuck all over his face. "I told Dunc this prince business would be a cinch."

Charles closed his eyes. "The car is waiting."

On the way to the Crystal Room, Charles explained Amos's duties. He would be the guest of honor at a reception given by the Daughters of Independence. He would be introduced to several ladies and their husbands. All he had to do was nod his head, shake hands, and say something appropriate—like good afternoon.

They were met at the door by a rather large woman wearing a formal gown and a sparkling tiara in her gray hair. She curtsied and said, "Ooh, Your Highness, we are so-oo delighted to have you."

Amos stuck out his hand. "Thanks, lady. I'm glad you asked me. It's not every day you get invited to a swank deal like this one."

The woman looked confused. "Uh, yes— well, please follow me, Your Highness."

She led him to the front of an elegantly furnished room. A long line of people had formed, waiting to meet him.

Amos nodded, said good afternoon, and shook one hundred and sixty-three hands. By the end, his hand felt like a ripe watermelon. It was swollen to three times its normal size.

Charles leaned over. "You're doing very well, sir."

Amos glared at him. "You didn't tell me I had to shake hands with everybody in the city."

The next woman curtsied, and Amos nodded, but he put his hand in his pocket.

A reporter was waiting at the end of the receiving line along with his cameraman. They flashed a couple of pictures and asked if the prince would be willing to answer a few questions.

"His Highness is quite fatigued. We will be leaving for the hotel at once." Charles took Amos's arm and propelled him toward the door.

The reporter followed. "I understand that Your Highness actually hates being in the United States and is rushing through this goodwill tour in an effort to return home as soon as possible?"

Amos stopped and turned. "I don't know where you get your information, bud, but I can honestly say that I'd rather be in the good old U.S. than anywhere else in the world."

The reporter was writing furiously. "Then why have you avoided most of your appointments with our state legislature?"

"Hey. You've got it backward. From what I hear, those guys in the capitol don't want to talk to me." Amos shrugged. "What can I say?"

Charles took his arm again and whispered, "I think you've said quite enough."

Chapter · 7

Dunc passed the prince in the hall of the capitol. "How's it going, Gus?"

"Not well. By now, I had hoped to locate some evidence of the conspiracy. So far, all I've done is run for coffee. How about you?"

"I'm on my way to Senator Grafter's office. He forgot his briefcase, and I have to get it for him. You can come with me if you want."

The prince looked relieved. "It sounds better than going for more coffee."

The senator's secretary unlocked the door. "Let me know when you boys are through in there. He likes to keep it locked up tight."

Dunc looked around. "The senator thought he left his briefcase on the floor by the coatrack. But I don't see it, do you?"

The prince walked around the desk. "Here it is." He picked up the leather case and started back around. The latch flew open, and papers went everywhere.

Dunc rubbed his chin. "You know, Gus, you and Amos may be more alike than you realize."

The prince knelt and started putting things back into the case. One of the papers caught his attention. "Dunc, look at this."

Dunc scanned the paper. "Now, why would a state senator have a letter in his briefcase about a possible oil strike in Moldavia?"

The secretary opened the door. "Are you boys having trouble?"

"No, ma'am. We just had a little accident. We'll have it picked up in no time." Dunc started stuffing things back into the briefcase.

"Here, I'll do that." The secretary picked

up a handful of the papers. "Senator Grafter sent word that he found the document he was looking for. He doesn't need his briefcase after all."

The prince shot Dunc a worried look.

Dunc reached over to help straighten the rest of the papers. "I was just wondering. What does the senator do when he's not here? I mean, what kind of job does he have?"

The secretary looked surprised. "At one time he was the president of his own oil company. Everyone knows that. But he resigned when he was elected senator, so there wouldn't be any conflict of interest. Now he completely devotes himself to serving the people who elected him."

"That's very interesting." Dunc headed for the door. "Well, we better get back. The senator may need us."

They walked down the hall and ducked into the nearest rest room. Dunc checked to make sure no one was listening. "I'd say we now have a major suspect."

The prince nodded. "Senator Grafter. It looks as if he's after our new oil strike. But what I don't understand is, why is he trying to discredit me in the bargain?"

Dunc tapped his chin. "Does your father have any enemies?"

"I'm sure he does. Most monarchs do. Why do you ask?"

"I don't think the senator is working alone. Someone from your country has to be feeding him information. Someone who wants to make you and your father look bad."

The prince drew himself to attention. "I'll have my country's special police force investigate this right away."

"Great. In the meantime we'll keep an eye on Senator Grafter."

"I wonder if we should call and check on Amos?" the prince asked.

Dunc smiled. "Amos isn't really good on phones. No, I think it would be better if we checked on him in person."

Chapter · 8

The doorbell rang. Amos waited for Charles to answer it. It rang again.

"Might as well make myself useful." Amos turned down the video game on the big-screen television and opened the door.

A woman wearing a brown fur around her neck bustled in. She planted a gushy kiss on Amos's cheek. "How are you, my dear nephew? Harold and I were bored, so we thought we'd drop in for a visit."

Amos wiped the wet kiss off his face. A boy a few years older than Amos marched in through the door behind the woman. He stood so straight and his nose was stuck so far in the air, Amos wondered how he could see where he was going. Three porters carrying bags and pushing carts with trunks on them followed the boy.

Charles stepped in from the kitchen. He was obviously not expecting them. "Lady Sophie, how . . . nice to see you. May I take your coat?"

"Of course you may take my coat, idiot. Do you think I want to wear it all day?" She threw the fur into Charles's arms.

Harold noticed the video game on the television. "What's this? Taken to playing children's games, Gustav? I would think a prince would have more important matters to attend to."

Amos looked at Charles. "I need to see you in the kitchen."

"Certainly, Your Highness."

Amos closed the door. "Who are these people?"

"They're your relatives. That is, they're Prince Gustav's relatives. His aunt Sophie and his first cousin Harold."

"Can we get rid of them?"

"I'm afraid it would be very bad form to

36

ask them to leave. They might suspect something."

Amos sulked. "Okay, but I'm going to finish my game. I didn't rack up all those points for nothing."

"As you wish, sir."

The doorbell rang, and Charles started for it. Amos stopped him. "I'll get it. You keep the relatives happy."

Sophie gave Amos a phony smile as he walked past. He pulled the door open. Dunc and the prince tried to step in. Amos's eyes widened, and he slammed the door. He looked at Sophie. "Room service. They have the wrong room."

The doorbell rang again. "I guess those guys just can't take no for an answer," Amos said. "I better go out and have a little talk with them."

He opened the door just wide enough to ease his body through and pulled it shut behind him.

"Are you crazy?" Dunc started. "You nearly—"

Amos held up his hand. "We've got trouble. The relatives from back home are here.

Aunt Sophie and Cousin Harold. From the looks of their suitcases, I'd say they're planning on staying awhile. Maybe we better switch back while there's still time."

The prince patted Amos's shoulder. "It won't be long now. I'm expecting an important call at your motel room from my chief security officer. Then we should be able to clear up this whole matter."

"What am I supposed to do with them?" Amos pointed at the penthouse door.

The prince grinned. "Do what I do—ignore them."

"You better get back inside before they get suspicious." Dunc moved to the elevator. "We'll get back to you as soon as we know anything."

Amos watched the elevator doors close. He took a deep breath and opened the door. Harold was turning off the television.

"What are you doing?" Amos yelled. "Do you realize it took me a full hour to get that score?"

"Surely you're joking," Harold sneered. "No one with any intelligence would waste their time with something as moronic as this."

"Oh, yeah? We'll see about that." Amos reached for the remote control. "I challenge you to a duel."

Chapter · 9

Charles turned on the overhead light in the living room. "Sir, it's two o'clock in the morning. You have an appointment in a few hours."

"Hold on one minute. . . . Yes! I win again." Amos stood up and stretched. He looked at his list of winnings. "Okay, Harold, time to pay up. You owe me your foxhunting horse, your motorcycle, your new white limousine, and your estate in Suffork. I'll take an IOU."

Harold scribbled on a piece of paper and handed it to Amos. "I can't believe I let you sucker me into playing this stupid game."

Amos gave the paper to Charles. "Don't be such a sore loser, Harold. Why don't you just admit you were up against the best and didn't have a chance?"

Harold put his nose in the air and stomped off to his room.

The corners of Charles's mouth turned up slightly. "Well done, sir."

"Thanks. I guess I better get some sleep. What's on the schedule for today?"

"I'll wake you at seven. We are visiting a group of schoolchildren."

Amos yawned. "I can handle that. Good night."

Seven o'clock came before Amos thought it had a right to. Charles called him, shook him, and finally ended up dragging him out of bed.

Amos stumbled into the kitchen, wearing the prince's pajamas. His hair stood up. He could open only one eye, and even it was having trouble.

Sophie was sitting at the kitchen table, reading a newspaper. She studied Amos over the top of the paper as a cat studies a mouse. "You seem different, nephew. I can't put my finger on it, but something isn't right."

Charles brought Amos's breakfast. "The United States has had a quite an effect on His Highness."

"So I see." She held up the front page. "You told a reporter you'd rather be here than anywhere else in the world. Does that include your own country?"

Amos rubbed his eyes and looked at the picture. "Hey, that's a good likeness. I've always wanted to be on the front page. Wait until I show the guys back home."

Charles cleared his throat. "It's time to get dressed for your appointment, Your Highness. We don't want to be late."

"Right." Amos slid off the chair and headed for his room. "I think I've got the hang of it, Chuck. I'll call you if I have trouble with that slingshot thing."

Sophie's eyes narrowed as she watched him leave the room.

Amos managed his clothes a little better this time. The only thing Charles had to do was slick down his hair.

The chauffeur held open the door of the

car while Charles and Amos stepped inside. Amos plopped on the leather seat. "What a relief to get away from that Sophie! How does the prince stand her?"

"The prince rarely has any contact with her. There have been hard feelings between the two families. Sophie is married to the king's brother, and for a while it looked as if her son, Harold, would be the heir to the throne. But then Prince Gustav was born and dashed her hopes. She has always resented him."

The car stopped in front of the capitol building. Amos started to get out. "I forgot to ask. What am I supposed to say to these little kids?"

Charles straightened Amos's tie. "Nod your head, shake hands, and—"

"I know," Amos said. "Say something appropriate—like good afternoon."

Charles smiled. "Very good, sir. Only it's morning."

"Whatever." Amos looked out the window. A familiar figure approached the car.

Chapter · 10

"Quick, hide!" Amos ducked down in the seat. "That's my teacher from school."

Mrs. Wormwood knocked on the car window. "Excuse me, Prince Gustav. The students are waiting." She knocked again. "Yoo-hoo, Prince."

Amos slid into the floor. "If she sees me, we're dead meat."

"May I offer a suggestion, sir?"

"Only if it has to do with catching a quick plane to Mexico."

"I think you should go through with it. She won't know you. You've fooled everyone so far—even the prince's own relatives."

Amos sat up. A little. "You don't know this woman. She has radar or something. Once, in the back of the room, Jimmy Farrel was making this pile of spit wads while she had her back turned. Out of the blue she stopped, went straight to Jimmy's desk, and made him eat every one of them. It was spooky."

Charles watched Mrs. Wormwood beat on the window. "I suppose we could cancel. But it wouldn't do the prince's reputation any good."

"You don't understand," Amos said. "If she catches me, she'll send what's left of me home in an envelope."

"Very well, sir. We'll call it off. After all, it's not your country or your reputation that some ruthless person is attempting to ruin. I can see why you would want to put your own personal problems before the welfare of an entire country."

Amos groaned. "Oh, all right, I'll do it. But Gus better appreciate this."

Charles signaled the chauffeur, who came around and opened the door for them.

Amos stepped out. He couldn't believe

his eyes. Mrs. Wormwood actually curtsied. He leaned over to Charles. "This definitely has possibilities."

She led them to the courtyard on the side of the building. Amos spotted Dunc and the prince waiting in the back of the line to shake his hand. The prince pulled Amos's ball cap down low. Dunc winked at him and grinned from ear to ear.

Amos played his part to perfection.

Almost.

He shook hands and said good morning to everyone in line until . . .

Melissa.

When she put out her hand, he froze. He turned bright red and forgot his line, his name, his life, how to breathe, think, see. Everything left him.

Charles elbowed him. Amos blinked. He gently took Melissa's hand, clicked his heels together, and bowed.

Melissa flashed him a brilliant smile.

A giggle went through the line. Mrs. Wormwood took out her fan and gasped, "Oh, my goodness."

The rest of the students shook his hand,

47

but Amos was totally unaware. All he could think of was that not only had he, Amos Binder, held Melissa Hansen's hand in his but she had smiled at him. It was a day for the history books. When he got home, he'd ask her to go steady, and then . . .

"Amos, pay attention," Dunc muttered furtively as he was shaking Amos's hand. "We need to talk."

Amos blinked again. "Did you see that, Dunc? She loves me."

"Keep your voice down." Dunc kept shaking his hand. "We have some new information. We'll meet you by the water fountain when this is over."

The prince shook Amos's hand quickly and moved to the other side of the garden so no one would notice anything.

When the last student had moved aside, Mrs. Wormwood took Amos's arm. "Tell me, Your Highness. Do you enjoy school?"

"I would probably enjoy school very much if it weren't for one thing."

"What is that, Your Highness?"

"I have an extremely disagreeable social studies teacher. She gives a mountain of

48

homework every night and insists on seating her students in alphabetical order. Have you ever heard of anything so ridiculous?"

"N-no," Mrs. Wormwood sputtered. "No, I haven't."

Chapter · 11

Amos bent over and pressed the button on the water fountain. Water squirted him in the face and soaked the front of his jacket. The purple banner across his chest faded onto his white shirt. He noticed the "out of order" sign just as Dunc walked up.

"What are you doing?" Dunc asked.

Amos looked down at his jacket. "It's a new method of cleaning clothes. I'll show it to you later."

"I think I'll pass. Where's Charles?"

"He went to find the chauffeur. Where's Gus?"

"He's keeping an eye on Senator Grafter."

"Why? I thought he was supposed to be working for Senator Suborn?"

"That's what I need to talk to you about. The prince's chief intelligence officer called last night. We found out that Senator Grafter is trying to buy the rights to a new oil field in Gus's country."

Amos pulled his arm out of the sleeve. "So?"

"The senator claims to have no connections with any oil company. If we can prove he does, then he's in big trouble."

Amos twisted the jacket and squeezed some of the water out. "You're going to get to the part that makes sense any minute now, right?"

"The intelligence officer says the senator is working with somebody from inside the country who wants to make the prince and his father look bad. Whoever it is, is trying to make it look like Gus and his dad are selling off the oil rights when the country needs them desperately."

Amos slipped the jacket back on. "Hmm. Seems a little smaller than it was before."

"Here's what we need you to do."

"I knew we'd get to this part," Amos said. "How weird is it this time?"

"It's not that bad. Really."

"You say that every time."

"This time I mean it. All you have to do is show up here tomorrow in the limousine and bring an extra suit of clothes for the prince."

"What's the catch?"

"There's no catch. Gus has a tape recorder, and we're going to keep following the senator. But even if we don't get any evidence, Gus is going to make a speech at two o'clock tomorrow to try to put a stop to what's going on."

"And all I have to do is show up and trade places with the prince?"

"That's it."

"Wait a minute. How come they're going to let Gus give a speech? I thought someone was keeping him off the list of speakers."

"Let's just say some very clever pages managed to put him back on the list."

"Are you guys working with someone else?"

"Very funny."

Amos shrugged. "Anything else I need to know?"

"We'll be waiting for you in the rest room on the second floor. Don't be late."

Chapter · 12

Dunc hid the tape recorder in the bottom of the trash can. He covered it with a couple of pieces of paper.

"Did you turn it on?" Gus asked.

Dunc nodded. "Full blast. We should be able to hear him breathe."

"I hope we get something. This is our last chance. I'd rather make that speech this afternoon with some solid evidence. Otherwise, it's just my word against his."

Dunc started for the door. "We better go. The secretary thinks we're in here on an errand for the senator. She might get suspicious."

"I heard her say she was going to lunch."

"Just the same, we better—shh, somebody's coming!" Dunc pointed to the closet. They scrambled in and closed the door.

The senator was talking to someone. "I don't know how it happened. I did everything I could to keep him off the speakers' list."

"That's not good enough," a woman hissed. "Our deal was for you to make him look bad. In return, I would make sure you had the top bid on those oil wells."

The prince's eyes widened. He leaned close to Dunc and whispered, "It's my aunt Sophie."

The woman continued, "If he gets back in the good graces of the people of Moldavia, I will hold you personally responsible. Our agreement will be terminated."

"You can't do that. My company needs those wells."

"Then I suggest you take whatever steps you find necessary to make him appear incompetent—or else. Do you understand?"

The senator sighed. "I understand."

"Good. I will be waiting for your report."

The woman's heels clicked against the floor as she left the room.

The senator sat at his desk for a few minutes. Then he gathered his things and followed her.

Dunc waited. He cautiously peeked out of the closet. "All clear."

The prince uncovered the tape recorder and smiled. "I can't believe our luck."

Dunc tried the door. "It's locked. We're locked in."

"Oh, no!" Gus looked at his watch. "We're supposed to meet Amos in fifteen minutes!"

Dunc moved to the window. "It's three stories to the ground. Any suggestions?"

Amos washed his hands five times. He looked at his teeth in the mirror and sat on the counter, holding the extra suit, and waited.

Charles opened the door. "Any sign of them?"

Amos shook his head. "I wonder what's keeping them. Gus is going to be late for his speech."

57

"I fear it may be foul play."

Amos slid off the counter. "What do you mean? You think somebody kidnaped them?"

"It's a possibility."

"What should we do?"

"First we need to cancel the speech. Then we'll check their motel room. If no one's heard from them, we may need to call the police."

"I'll go up and cancel the speech," Amos said. "You get the chauffeur to bring the car around."

Amos hung the suit on the back of the bathroom door and headed for the elevator. When he stepped out, a young man was waiting for him. "This way, Your Highness. You have less than a minute."

Amos followed him through some double doors. "Wait. I don't think you understand. See, I need to talk to someone about—"

Amos stopped and looked around. He was on the senate floor. Everyone stood and applauded.

When they sat down, the room was deathly silent. Amos thought about making a run for it. He chewed his lip and looked up at the sea of faces in the gallery.

He moved to the podium and tapped the microphone. "Um, hello there. I'm—well, you all know who I am. What I'd like to know is who you are."

A ripple of laughter passed through the audience.

"Never mind. I can see your nameplates on your desks. Hey—you guys have to sit in alphabetical order too."

Another ripple of laughter.

Amos waited. The people were smiling. He was a hit. Maybe he should really go for it. He put his hand inside his jacket and puffed out his chest. "Four score and seven years ago . . ."

"Psst!" Dunc was waving at him from the door.

Amos bent down to the mike. "Hold that thought. Excuse me for just a minute."

Dunc grabbed him as he opened the door, and the real prince stepped back onto the stage.

Chapter · 13

Amos stepped back from the mirror. He had just spent twenty minutes slicking his hair back. "Well, what do you think—do I have it right?"

They were back at Dunc's house, in Dunc's bedroom. Dunc was unpacking. Amos had decided to wait to unpack until later. Maybe next year.

"It depends. What are you trying to look like—a greaseball?" Dunc put his socks in the drawer.

"I'm trying to look like the prince. I thought I'd go over and impress Melissa.

You know, do the bowing and hand-holding routine again."

"Amos, we promised Gus we wouldn't tell anybody about you taking his place."

"I wasn't going to actually tell her. I thought I'd repeat some of my awesome speech and see if she noticed on her own."

Dunc laughed. "That was Abraham Lincoln's speech. And besides, you barely got started. Gus is the one who gave the awesome speech. Thanks to him, the police have Senator Grafter in custody and Gus's aunt Sophie is in disgrace."

"He did all right, I guess. But it was because I had the audience warmed up. If you guys hadn't shown up—"

"If we hadn't shown up, you would have been in big trouble. I hope Charles is okay. That coatrack I threw out the window hit him pretty hard."

"He's okay. But he'll probably walk with a limp for a while. You had to do it. Otherwise he wouldn't have noticed you and found a janitor to let you out of Senator Grafter's office."

Dunc nodded. "I suppose."

Amos added a handful of grease to his hair until it was a half-inch or so thick, then started for the door. "Well, wish me luck."

Dunc thought about telling him that Melissa wouldn't let him into her house, much less let him hold her hand. He thought about telling Amos that Melissa only smiled for princes. He thought about a lot of things he could say. But instead he just smiled.

"Good luck, Amos."

Be sure to join Dunc and Amos in these other Culpepper Adventures:

The Case of the Dirty Bird

When Dunc Culpepper and his best friend, Amos, first see the parrot in a pet store, they're not impressed—it's smelly, scruffy, and missing half its feathers. They're only slightly impressed when they learn that the parrot speaks four languages, has outlived ten of its owners, and is probably 150 years old. But when the bird starts mouthing off about buried treasure, Dunc and Amos get pretty excited—let the amateur sleuthing begin!

Dunc's Doll

Dunc and his accident-prone friend Amos are up to their old sleuthing habits once again. This time they're after a band of doll thieves! When a doll that once belonged to Charles Dickens's daughter is stolen from an exhibition at the local mall, the two boys put on their detective gear and do some serious snooping. Will a vicious watchdog keep them from retrieving the valuable missing doll?

Culpepper's Cannon

Dunc and Amos are researching the Civil War cannon that stands in the town square when they find a note inside telling them about a time portal. Entering it through the dressing room of La Petite, a women's clothing store, the boys find themselves in downtown Chatham on March 8, 1862—the day before the historic clash between the *Monitor* and the *Merrimac*. But the Confederate soldiers they meet mistake them for Yankee spies. Will they make it back to the future in one piece?

Dunc Gets Tweaked

Dunc and Amos meet up with a new buddy named Lash when they enter the radical world of skateboard competition. When somebody "cops"—steals—Lash's prototype skateboard, the boys are determined to get it back. After all, Lash is about to shoot for a totally rad world's record! Along the way they learn a major lesson: *Never* kiss a monkey!

Dunc's Halloween

Dunc and Amos are planning the best route to get the most candy on Halloween. But their plans change when Amos is slightly bitten by a werewolf. He begins scratching himself and chasing UPS trucks—he's become a werepuppy!

Dunc Breaks the Record

Dunc and Amos have a small problem when they try hang gliding—they crash in the wilderness. Luckily, Amos has read a book about a boy who survived in the wilderness for fifty-four days. Too bad Amos doesn't have a hatchet. Things go from bad to worse when a wild man holds the boys captive. Can anything save them now?

Dunc and the Flaming Ghost

Dunc's not afraid of ghosts, although Amos is sure that the old Rambridge house is haunted by the ghost of Blackbeard the Pirate. Then the best friends meet Eddie, a meek man who claims to be impersonating Blackbeard's ghost in order to live in the house in peace. But if that's true, why are flames shooting from his mouth?

Amos Gets Famous

Deciphering a code they find in a library book, Amos and Dunc stumble onto a burglary ring. The burglars' next target is the home of Melissa, the girl of Amos's dreams (who doesn't even know that he's alive). Amos longs to be a hero to Melissa, so nothing will stop him from solving this case—not even a mind-boggling collision with a jock, a chimpanzee, and a toilet.

Dunc and Amos Hit the Big Top

In order to impress Melissa, Amos decides to perform on the trapeze at the visiting circus. Look out below! But before Dunc can talk him out of his plan, the two stumble across a mystery behind the scenes at the circus. Now Amos is in double trouble. What's really going on under the big top?

Dunc's Dump

Camouflaged as piles of rotting trash, Dunc and Amos are sneaking around the town dump. Dunc wants to find out who is polluting the garbage at the dump with hazardous and toxic waste. Amos just wants to impress Melissa. Can either of them succeed?

Dunc and the Scam Artists

Dunc and Amos are at it again. Some older residents of their town have been bilked by con artists, and the two boys want to look into these crimes. They meet elderly Betsy Dell, whose nasty nephew Frank gives the boys the creeps. Then they notice some soft dirt in Ms. Dell's shed, and a shovel. Does Frank have something horrible in store for Dunc and Amos?

Dunc and Amos and the Red Tattoos

Dunc and Amos head for camp and face two weeks of fresh air—along with regulations, demerits, KP, and inedible food. But where these two best friends go, trouble follows. They overhear a threat against the camp director and discover that camp funds have been stolen. Do these crimes have anything to do with the tattoo of the exotic red flower that some of the camp staff have on their arms?

Dunc's Undercover Christmas

It's Christmastime! and Dunc, Amos, and Amos's cousin T.J. hit the mall for some serious shopping. But when the seasonal magic is threatened by some disappearing presents, and Santa Claus himself is a prime suspect, the

boys put their celebration on hold and go under-
cover in perfect Christmas disguises! Can the
sleuthing trio protect Santa's threatened reputation and catch the impostor before he strikes
again?

The Wild Culpepper Cruise

When Amos wins a "Why I Love My Dog" con-
test, he and Dunc are off on the Caribbean
cruise of their dreams! But there's something
downright fishy about Amos's suitcase and before they know it, the two best friends wind up
with more high-seas adventure than they bar-
gained for. Can Dunc and Amos figure out
who's out to get them and salvage what's left of
their vacation?

Dunc and the Haunted Castle

When Dunc and Amos are invited to spend a
week in Scotland, Dunc can already hear the
bagpipes a-blowin'. But when the boys spend
their first night in an ancient castle, it isn't
bagpipes they hear. It's moans! Dunc hears
groaning coming from inside his bedroom walls.
Amos notices the eyes of a painting follow him
across the room! Could the castle really be
haunted? Local legend has it that the castle's

former lord wanders the ramparts at night in search of his head! Team up with Dunc and Amos as they go ghostbusting in the Scottish Highlands!

Cowpokes and Desperadoes

Git along, little dogies! Dunc and Amos are bound for Uncle Woody Culpepper's Santa Fe cattle ranch for a week of fun. But when they overhear a couple of cowpokes plotting to do Uncle Woody in, the two sleuths are back on the trail of some serious action! Who's been making off with all the prize cattle? Can Dunc and Amos stop the rustlers in time to save the ranch?

CULPEPPER ADVENTURES

Gary Paulsen

Dunc Culpepper and Amos Binder are best friends—and
they always get into trouble. Follow the fast-paced
mystery adventures of the sleuthing trio and get in on all
the fun as they get themselves in—and out of—trouble.

☐	40598-X	**The Case of the Dirty Bird**	$3.25/$3.99 Can.
☐	40601-3	**Dunc's Doll**	$3.25/$3.99 Can.
☐	40617-X	**Culpepper's Cannon**	$3.25/$3.99 Can.
☐	40642-0	**Dunc Gets Tweaked**	$3.25/$3.99 Can.
☐	40659-5	**Dunc's Halloween**	$3.25/$3.99 Can.
☐	40678-1	**Dunc's Journey to the Center of the Earth (Nov. 92)**	$3.25/$3.99 Can.
☐	40686-2	**Dunc and the Flaming Ghost**	$3.25/$3.99 Can.
☐	40749-4	**Amos Gets Famous**	$3.25/$3.99 Can.
☐	40756-7	**Dunc and Amos Hit the Big Top**	$3.25/$3.99 Can.
☐	40762-1	**Dunc's Dump**	$3.25/$3.99 Can.
☐	40775-3	**Dunc and the Scam Artists**	$3.25/$3.99 Can.
☐	40790-7	**Dunc and Amos and the Red Tattoos**	$3.25/$3.99 Can.

Buy them at your local bookstore or use this
page for ordering.

BOOKS FOR YOUNG READERS,
2451 S. Wolf Road,
Des Plaines, IL 60018

Bantam Doubleday Dell
Books for Young Readers

Please send me the items I have checked above. I am enclosing
$_____ (please add $2.50 to cover postage and handling).
Send check or money order, no cash or C.O.D.s please.

MR./MS. _____

ADDRESS _____

CITY _____ STATE _____ ZIP _____

Please allow four to six weeks for delivery.
Prices and availability subject to change without notice.